FOR
KELSEY

SIMON & SCHUSTER BOOKS FOR YOUNG READERS
An imprint of Simon & Schuster Children's Publishing Division
1230 Avenue of the Americas, New York, New York 10020
SIMON & SCHUSTER BOOKS FOR YOUNG READERS is a trademark of Simon & Schuster, Inc.
For information about special discounts for bulk purchases, please contact
Simon & Schuster Special Sales at 1-866-506-1949 or business@simonandschuster.com.
The Simon & Schuster Speakers Bureau can bring authors to your live event.
For more information or to book an event, contact the Simon & Schuster Speakers Bureau
at 1-866-248-3049 or visit our website at www.simonspeakers.com.
Book design by Lucy Ruth Cummins
The text for this book is set in Typewriter.
The illustrations for this book are rendered in pencil and watercolor, and assembled digitally.
Manufactured in China
0416 SCP
2 4 6 8 10 9 7 5 3 1
Library of Congress Cataloging-in-Publication Data
Clanton, Ben, 1988– author.
It came in the mail / Ben Clanton. — First edition.
pages cm
Summary: After Liam writes to his mailbox, asking for more mail, he gets his wish,
but soon he realizes that sending mail is even more fun than receiving it.
ISBN 978-1-4814-0360-3 (hardcover : alk. paper)—ISBN 978-1-4814-0361-0 (eBook)
1. Mailboxes—Juvenile fiction. 2. Postal service—Juvenile fiction. [1. Mailboxes—Fiction.
2. Postal service—Fiction.] I. Title.
PZ7.C52923It 2016
[E]—dc23
2014043694

IT CAME IN THE MAIL

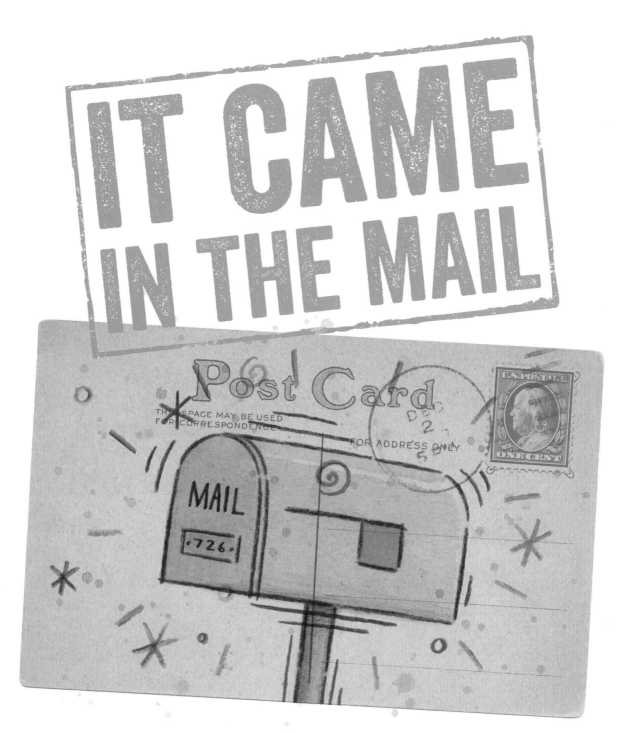

Post Card

THIS SPACE MAY BE USED FOR CORRESPONDENCE

FOR ADDRESS ONLY

U.S. POSTAGE
ONE CENT

MAIL
·726·

Ben Clanton

Simon & Schuster Books for Young Readers

New York   London   Toronto   Sydney   New Delhi

Liam loved to get mail.

Too bad he never got any.

He checked ~~daily~~

 ~~hourly~~

every few seconds,
but found . . .

. . . diddly-squat.

But then, on a day much like any other,
an idea struck Liam.

If he sent some mail,
then maybe he'd get some in return.

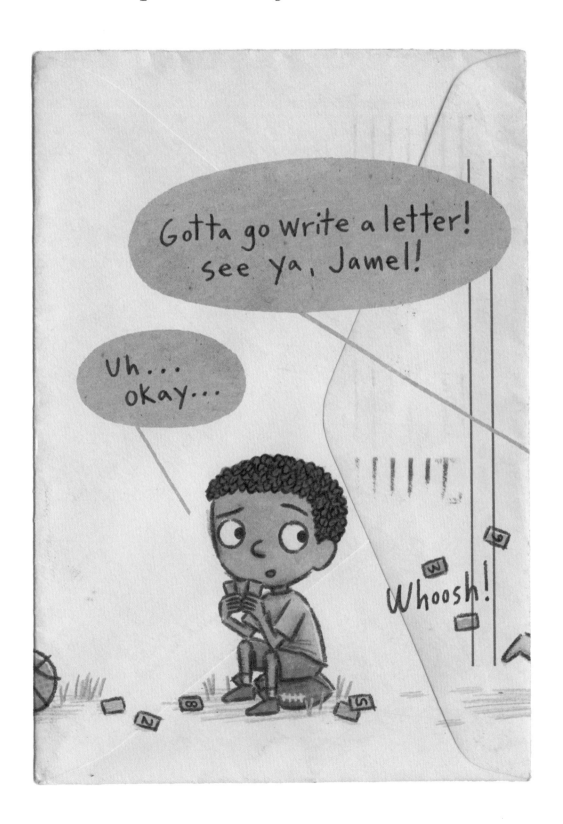

Not sure who to send something to,
Liam sent a letter to his mailbox.

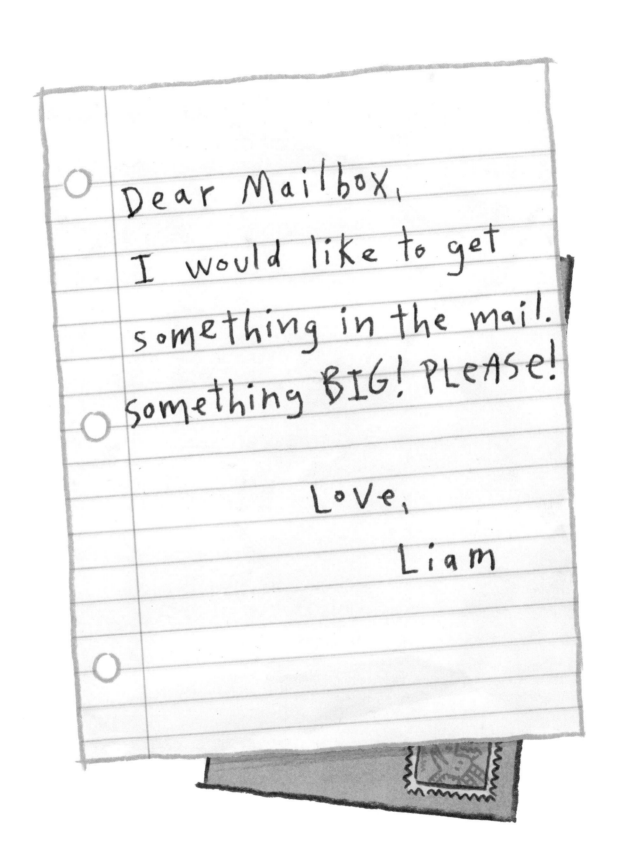

As soon as Liam put the letter in,
the mailbox began to shake.
It made all sorts of strange sounds.

KRINK

When Liam looked inside,
he was met by a blast of fire.
A dragon had come in the mail!

And it was for Liam.

Liam loved the dragon.
But he couldn't wait to see what
he might get next!

Dear Mailbox,

Thank you for the
fire-breathing dragon.
It is just what I
always wanted.
Can you send me more
stuff? PLEASE!
        Love,
            Liam
P.S. You are the best
    mailbox ever!

Soon the mailbox was spitting
out all sorts of things.
Pickles! Pigs! A whale with wings!
A trombone! A triceratops bone!
Even a funny bone!

Liam liked it all!
He liked it all so much
that he wanted even more.

Oodles and oodles of mail
flooded out of the mailbox.

What was Liam to do with it all?!

And then another idea struck Liam.

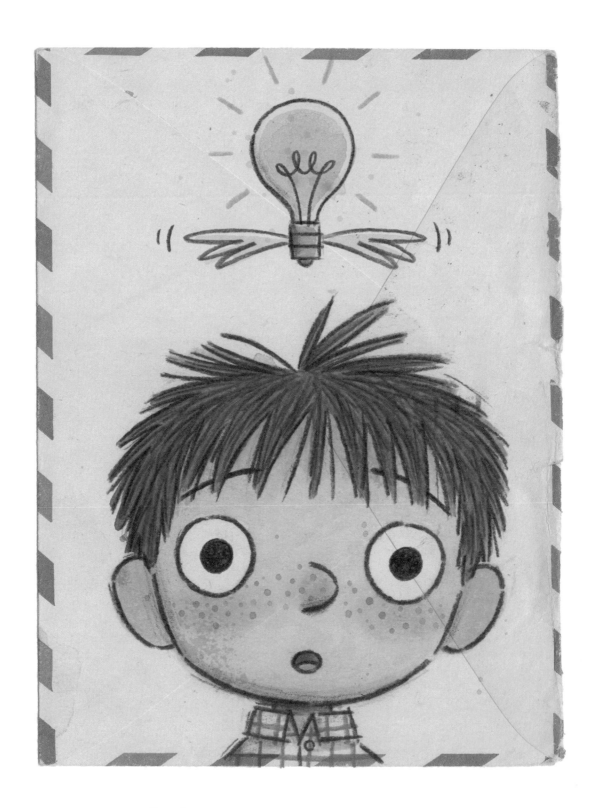

He probably wasn't the only kid
who had ever wanted to get mail.

Dear Mailbox,

Thank you for ALL the mail! ~~the~~ But I think it's maybe too much for just me. Can you help me send some of it to other kids?

Love,
Liam

With some help from the mailbox . . .

. . . Liam was soon mailing things

to kids all over the place!

Liam found he rather liked sending stuff.
He liked it so much that before long,
almost everything was gone.

That was okay with Liam.
He could always ask the
mailbox for more. . . .